A Note from Michelle about FOR THE BIRDS

Hi! I'm Michelle Tanner. I'm nine years old, and I've got a problem. Rachel Tilly and I saw a rare bird called the Cassin's finch. It's a very rare bird. Everyone made a big deal over it. We got our picture in the newspaper. People were even calling us heroes! But then I found out we made a huge mistake. The bird we saw was really a house finch—and there are lots of those in San Francisco.

I think we should tell the truth. But Rachel wants to try her secret plan first. I can't even tell my family about it. And that's not going to be easy because I live in a very full house!

There's my dad and my two older sisters, D.J. and Stephanie. But that's not all.

My mom died when I was little. So my uncle Jesse moved in to help Dad take care of us. So did Joey Gladstone. He's my dad's friend from college. It's almost like having three dads. But that's still not all!

First Uncle Jesse got married to Becky Donaldson. Then they had twin boys, Nicky and Alex. The twins are four years old now. And they're so cute.

That's nine people. And our dog, Comet, makes ten. Sure, it gets kind of crazy sometimes. But I wouldn't change it for anything. It's so much fun living in a full house!

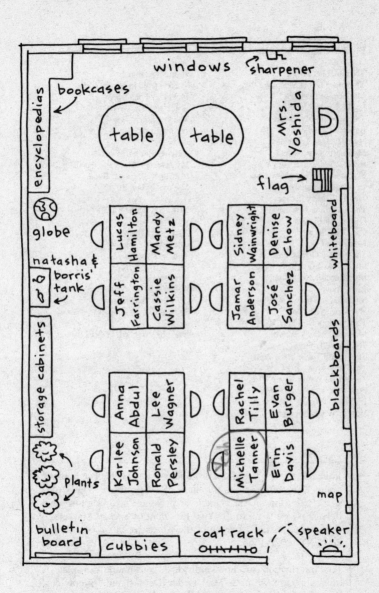

windows

sharpener

bookcases

encyclopedias

Mrs. Yoshida

table   table

flag

globe

Lucas Hamilton   Mandy Metz

Sidney Wainwright   Denise Chow

natasha & borris' tank

Jeff Farrington   Cassie Wilkins

Jamar Anderson   José Sanchez

whiteboard

storage cabinets

Anna Abdul   Lee Wagner

Rachel Tilly   Evan Burger

blackboards

plants

Karlee Johnson   Ronald Persley

Michelle Tanner   Erin Davis

map

bulletin board

cubbies

coat rack

speaker

FULL HOUSE™ MICHELLE novels

Available from MINSTREL Books

FULL HOUSE™

Michelle
and Friends

FOR THE BIRDS

Jacqueline Carrol

A Parachute Press Book

Published by POCKET BOOKS
New York   London   Toronto   Sydney   Singapore

A MINSTREL PAPERBACK *Original*

A Minstrel Book published by
POCKET BOOKS, a division of Simon & Schuster, Inc.
1230 Avenue of the Americas, New York, NY 10020

A PARACHUTE PRESS BOOK

Copyright © and ™ 2001 by Warner Bros.

FULL HOUSE, characters, names and all related indicia are
trademarks of Warner Bros. © 2001.

ISBN: 0-671-04202-5

First Minstrel Books printing March 2001

10   9   8   7   6   5   4   3   2   1

A MINSTREL BOOK and colophon are registered trademarks of
Simon & Schuster, Inc.

Printed in the U.S.A.

FOR THE BIRDS

Chapter

1

♥ "I love springtime," nine-year-old Michelle Tanner said to her best friends, Cassie Wilkins and Mandy Metz. It was Friday morning. The three friends were walking through the hall of Fraser Street Elementary School toward their classroom. Michelle sniffed the colorful bouquet she was holding. "And I love flowers, too."

"Mrs. Yoshida is really going to like those," Cassie said.

"Yeah," Mandy agreed. "It was nice of you to think of giving them to her."

"Thanks," Michelle said, smiling. "We have lots of flowers in our garden, so my dad said it was okay for me to pick some."

As they got closer to their classroom, a loud chirping noise filled the hall.

"Listen to all those birds!" Mandy cried. "Wow!"

Mrs. Yoshida was teaching a special unit on birds that week. She had told everyone they could bring their pet birds to class for the day. Mrs. Yoshida was even going to bring her pet dove, Daisy.

"Let's go see them," Michelle said.

Michelle, Mandy, and Cassie hurried into their classroom. On top of Lucas Hamilton's desk was a birdcage with a bright blue parakeet in it. Denise Chow's two tiny parakeets were fluttering around in their cage. Mrs.

Yoshida's plump gray dove sat in a cage on the teacher's desk.

But nobody was paying much attention to the dove or the parakeets. Everyone was gathered around Rachel Tilly's desk, staring at her big white cockatoo.

"What a cool bird," Michelle said. She walked to her desk, which was next to Rachel's. "What's its name?"

"Arthur. And don't stand too close to the cage," Rachel warned. "If he gets nervous, he won't talk."

"He can talk?" Jeff Farrington asked. "My aunt has a cockatoo, but it doesn't say anything."

Rachel tossed back her long brown hair. "Well, Arthur is very smart," she bragged.

Mandy rolled her eyes at Michelle. Rachel was always bragging about something.

"Arthur can say my name," Rachel told Jeff.

"Cool. Let's hear him," Jeff said.

Rachel bent down and put her face close to Arthur's cage. "Hi, Arthur," she said in a clear voice. "Say hello to Rachel. Hello, Rachel."

Arthur cocked his head and peered at her with his bright black eyes. "Hello, Rachel," he squawked.

Everyone laughed. Arthur fluttered his wings and squawked again. "Hello, Rachel . . . hello, Rachel!"

"See? I told you he was smart," Rachel said.

Mrs. Yoshida smiled. "He's great, Rachel. Thanks for bringing him."

"Mrs. Yoshida." Michelle held out the bunch of flowers. "I picked these for you this morning."

Mrs. Yoshida was very pleased. "Thank you, Michelle. I'll put them in water and set them on my desk so everyone can enjoy them." She walked toward the door. "I'll be back in a minute, everybody. Then I have some slides to show you."

Rachel smirked at Michelle. "You don't have a bird, do you? That's why you brought those flowers."

"Huh?" Michelle asked. What was Rachel talking about?

"You knew everybody would be paying attention to the birds," Rachel said. "I bet you're jealous because you don't have one, especially a cool one like Arthur. So you had to bring something to make Mrs. Yoshida pay attention to you."

Michelle couldn't believe it. She was not jealous of Rachel's bird. But before she could say anything, Mrs. Yoshida came back in and told everyone to sit down.

Rachel hurried off and put her cage on one of the round tables at the side of the room.

"Rachel's the jealous one," Cassie whispered to Michelle. "You were thinking of Mrs. Yoshida. Rachel was only thinking of herself."

"As usual," Mandy added.

Rachel came back and sat down. She was still smirking, but Michelle felt better after what Cassie and Mandy had said. She was lucky to have such good friends. Who cared what Rachel thought?

"All right, class," Mrs. Yoshida said. "For the next few days, we're going to be studying birds. We all know about parakeets and doves and even cockatoos."

Arthur squawked, and the class laughed.

"We have them for pets," Mrs. Yoshida went on. "But what about some of the wild birds that live around San Francisco? Or the birds that stop here on their way to somewhere else? Can you name some of them?"

"Robins," Erin called out.

"Bluejays," Evan Burger said.

"Sparrows," Mandy volunteered. "And . . . woodpeckers!"

Michelle tried to think of more birds, but she couldn't. She loved to hear them chirping outside, but she never bothered to find out what kind they were. Birds were just birds.

"It's surprising how many different kinds of wild birds there are around San Francisco," Mrs. Yoshida said. "Let's take a look at some of them. Erin, would you shut the lights off? And Lucas, you close the window blinds."

Mrs. Yoshida went to the back of the room and turned on the slide projector.

When the room was dark, the pet birds settled down. The fluttering and chirping stopped. Arthur squawked once and then grew quiet.

The first slide came up on the whiteboard at the front of the room.

7

"That's just a duck," Rachel said.

"It looks like one, but it's really a loon," Mrs. Yoshida told the class. "Loons are called diving birds because they dive under water for fish."

The second slide appeared. This bird had a black tail, back, and wings, with yellow on its chest and a bright red head. "This is a western tanager," Mrs. Yoshida said. "Tanagers eat harmful insects. And they also love cherries."

It's so pretty, Michelle thought.

The slide show continued. Except for a few of them, such as the hawks and gulls, Michelle didn't recognize a single one. She was amazed at how many different kinds there were. I guess birds aren't just birds, she thought.

"That was great," Mandy said when the slide show ended. "I'm definitely going to check out some birds on my way home."

"You must have read my mind." Mrs. Yoshida laughed. "That's your assignment, class. I want you to do a little bird-watching over the weekend. Sketch five different birds you see. A friend of mine is a member of the San Francisco Bird-Watchers Club. He's going to come in on Monday to see if he can identify the birds you draw."

Weekend homework was not exactly Michelle's favorite thing. But bird-watching would be more fun than work. She and Cassie and Mandy could make a picnic lunch and spend the whole next day at the park looking for birds.

"It'll be easier if you work with partners," Mrs. Yoshida went on. "So I'm going to pair you off. Cassie, you go with Lee."

Michelle was disappointed. Well, maybe she'd get paired with Mandy. The two of them could still have a picnic with Cassie and Lee.

Mrs. Yoshida went on picking partners. Michelle felt even more disappointed when Mandy and Denise were assigned to work together. What about me? she wondered. She glanced around and spotted Sidney Wainwright, Rachel's best friend.

"Michelle and . . ." Mrs. Yoshida began.

Not Sidney, Michelle thought. She's almost as bad as Rachel. Please, please, not Sidney.

"Michelle and Rachel," Mrs. Yoshida said.

Chapter
2

♥ Oh, no! Michelle thought. Out of all the kids in class, why did I have to get paired up with Rachel Tilly?

Michelle sneaked a peek at Rachel, who had a sour look on her face. She's not exactly crazy about me, either, Michelle thought.

Michelle and Rachel had never been friends. Rachel was very bossy and not very nice. Since Michelle had beaten her in the election for class president, Rachel hardly spoke to her anymore.

That was fine with Michelle. But now she'd have to spend hours bird-watching with Rachel! Michelle sighed loudly.

"I guess we're stuck with each other," Rachel complained.

"I guess so," Michelle whispered back unhappily.

Rachel sighed. "Okay. We might as well just get it over with. There are about a million trees in my backyard—and a zillion birds. Plus my dad just finished building me a really cool tree house. Come over tomorrow morning. We can sit in the tree house and check out the birds."

"Okay," Michelle agreed. It won't be as much fun as going to the park with my friends, she thought. But I guess I don't have any choice.

"Come early," Rachel added. "Like around seven. The backyard sounds like a bird party then."

Sitting in a tree house with Rachel on Saturday morning isn't my idea of a party, Michelle grumbled to herself. What an awful way to start the weekend!

Michelle felt grumpy for the rest of the day. By the time she got home, she was in a terrible mood. Comet, the family's golden retriever, took one look at her face and tucked his tail between his legs.

"I'm sorry, Comet," Michelle murmured. She dropped her backpack on the floor and patted the dog's head. "I'm not mad at you."

Comet wagged his tail happily. He trotted after her as she went into the kitchen.

Michelle's father, Danny, was sitting at the kitchen table, making a grocery list. "Hi, honey—whoa! What's with the grouchy expression?"

Michelle pulled out a chair and sat down

across from him. Comet flopped on the floor and put his chin on her feet. "Wouldn't you be grouchy if you had to go bird-watching with Rachel Tilly?" she asked.

Danny pushed his grocery list aside. "Come on, Michelle. Working with Rachel can't be *that* terrible, right?"

Michelle plopped her chin in her hands. "Yes, it can." She told her father all about Rachel. About halfway through, she stopped short.

"What's the matter?" Danny asked.

"I just noticed something strange," she said. "I've been talking for over five minutes, and no one has come along to interrupt me."

"You're right." Danny laughed. "That doesn't happen often."

Michelle lived in a very full house. Besides Michelle, Danny, and Comet, there were Michelle's sisters, Stephanie and D.J.

Stephanie was in eighth grade, and D.J. was in college.

Then there were Uncle Jesse and his wife, Becky. They lived on the third floor of the house with their four-year-old twins, Nicky and Alex. Joey Gladstone, Danny's best friend, lived in an apartment in the basement.

Michelle loved being part of such a big family. But it was nice to talk to her father alone, too. Especially when something was wrong. "Being stuck with Rachel is going to ruin my whole weekend," she complained.

"Only if you let it," Danny told her. "Besides, maybe Rachel isn't so bad."

Michelle stared at him. "Are you kidding?"

Danny shook his head. "You've never really spent any time with her. Now you have to. So why not try to get to know her? If you give it a chance, you might find out she isn't the awful person you think she is."

Michelle frowned. "Do you really think so?"

"It's worth a try," Danny said. "Don't you think?"

"I guess," Michelle agreed. "I mean, how bad can hanging out with Rachel be?"

Chapter 3

♥ Early the next morning Michelle let herself through the gate into Rachel's big backyard. Around her neck she wore a pair of binoculars Joey had lent her. She carried her sketch pad and a box of colored pencils.

"I'm up here!" Rachel's voice called out.

Michelle glanced around. Rachel stared down at her from a small house built on the branches of a huge oak tree. A wooden ladder leaned against the tree trunk. "Come on up," Rachel said.

Michelle tucked her pad and pencils under one arm and climbed the ladder.

The tree house had a slanted roof, a thick rug, and a bunch of fat pillows to sit on. On one side was a shelf with a portable CD player and a bunch of CDs.

"Wow, this is really cool," Michelle said. "Have you slept up here yet?"

Rachel shook her head. "It still gets too cold at night. But as soon as it's warm enough, I'm going to have lots of slumber parties."

"That'll be fun." Of course, she won't invite me, Michelle thought. Not that I would go.

Rachel yawned. Then she shivered. "It's so early that it's still cold. I brought up some cocoa for us." She pointed toward a big thermos next to the CDs.

Wow! Rachel had thought of somebody

besides herself! Michelle was amazed. It must have been a mistake.

Then she remembered what she'd told her father. I have to give Rachel a chance, she reminded herself.

Rachel poured two cups of steaming cocoa. She handed one to Michelle.

"Thanks," Michelle said. She took a sip.

The two girls drank some cocoa and then settled down to watch for birds.

They didn't have to wait long. A wood-pecker with a red chest landed in a nearby tree.

Michelle peered through the binoculars. She studied the bird for a few moments. Then she lowered the binoculars. She drew an out-line of the bird and then colored it in.

"There's another kind of bird," Rachel announced. She leaned back and yawned. "It's in the same tree, but it's higher up. I think it might be a crow. You should draw that one, too."

Michelle looked. The big, glossy black bird perched on a high branch and cocked its head to eye the ground below. Almost before Michelle finished sketching it, Rachel yawned and pointed out another bird.

This isn't fair, Michelle thought. I'm doing all the sketching. Rachel is just pointing out the birds and yawning a lot.

"Why don't you draw for a while?" Michelle suggested. "I don't think I should do it all."

"But you're so good at it," Rachel told her. "You're even a better artist than I am."

"Really?" Michelle asked.

"Really," Rachel said. "I've always liked the way you draw. With your artwork, our project is going to be the best one in class."

Michelle liked to draw. And she enjoyed the

compliment. But it sounded so strange coming from Rachel. Rachel usually thought she was the best at everything.

Wait until Mandy and Cassie hear about this, Michelle thought.

Rachel pointed out another bird. As Michelle lifted the binoculars, she decided that her father was right. Maybe she should try to get to know Rachel better. She might even invite her home after they finished. . . .

"Oh, no!" Rachel gasped.

"What's wrong?"

Rachel tapped her watch. "I'm supposed to meet Sidney at her house in fifteen minutes," she said. "Her parents are taking us on a picnic, and they wanted to get an early start. You have to leave right now, Michelle."

"Let me draw this bird first," Michelle said. "We're supposed to do five, remember? Just give me a second."

"Hurry!" Rachel cried. "I don't want to be late."

At the sound of Rachel's loud voice, the bird flapped its wings and took off.

"Did you get it?" Rachel demanded.

Michelle shook her head. "You scared it away."

Rachel groaned. Then she narrowed her eyes and peered around the yard. "There's one. It's sitting on top of the back fence. Right in the middle. See it?"

Michelle took a quick look through the binoculars. She saw a small, dark brown bird with red on its head, throat, back, and chest. She dropped the binoculars and flipped to a fresh page on her sketch pad.

"I really have to go," Rachel said as Michelle began to sketch the little bird. "Can't you draw any faster?"

"If I do, it will look terrible and our project

won't be any good," Michelle told her. She gritted her teeth and tried to ignore Rachel. She picked up a red pencil and started coloring. Just as she finished the head and throat, the pencil point snapped off.

Rachel groaned again. Michelle looked through her pencils. But there were no more red ones. Michelle groaned, too. "I guess we'll have to find another bird to draw."

"Are you kidding?" Rachel cried. "Just finish the sketch with a regular black pencil. Nobody will notice."

"Good idea," Michelle said. Anything to get out of here, she thought. She quickly shaded in the rest of the bird with a regular pencil. "Done!" she announced.

"Finally. Okay, I've got to really hurry now." Rachel scrambled down the ladder and ran toward her house.

Talk about rude, Michelle thought. First she

rushes me while I'm trying to draw. Then she runs off without even saying good-bye. *Rachel knew we had to do this,* Michelle thought angrily. *She shouldn't have made plans with Sidney.*

Michelle checked her watch. If she hurried, she could catch Mandy and Cassie before they left for the park. They were going there to do their bird projects with Denise and Lee.

I'll sketch the rest of my birds with them, Michelle decided. *It'll be fun to be with my friends, especially after spending the morning with Rachel.*

Michelle climbed down from the tree house and walked out of Rachel's yard. *I'm glad that partnership is over,* she thought. And she hurried away without looking back at the tree house even once.

Chapter
4

♥   "Who's that?" Rachel asked Michelle at school Monday morning. She pointed to a dark-haired man who was talking with Mrs. Yoshida at the front of the classroom.

"That must be the bird man," Michelle said. "Mrs. Yoshida told us she had a friend who would come talk about bird-watching, remember?"

"Oh, right. And he's going to look at our drawings, too," Rachel said. "You didn't forget them, I hope."

"No way." Michelle showed her a folder. It was red, with both of their names printed neatly on the cover. Inside were the three bird sketches she had done in the tree house Saturday morning, plus the other two she'd done later that day.

"Those are really good," Rachel said. "Much better than I could have done. I told you ours would be the best project in the class."

Michelle wasn't sure how she felt about that. She'd been angry that Rachel had left her to do all the work. But maybe Rachel had just figured they would get a better grade if Michelle did the drawing. It made sense in a way.

"All right, class, it's time to take your seats," Mrs. Yoshida called out. Everyone sat down. First Mrs. Yoshida collected their folders of bird sketches. Then she introduced the man she had been talking to.

"This is Mr. Simon, class," she said. "He's been a bird-watcher for a long time and knows a lot about birds. Today he will talk to you about them and look at some of your sketches."

Everyone clapped as Mr. Simon walked to the front of the room. "I'm really glad to be here," he said to the class. "Mrs. Yoshida told me that you went bird-watching over the weekend. How did you like it?"

"It was cool," Lucas said. "Except I didn't see any of the special birds we saw in the slide show on Friday."

"Me, either," Evan said. "And I got bored standing around staring up at the trees."

"Well, you should try standing near the ocean on a cold February morning, looking for a black oystercatcher." Mr. Simon laughed. "People bird-watch for lots of reasons. Some of them want to keep track of endangered species, and that's important. Some of us just love birds. And when a birder spots a bird that nobody ever sees, it's very exciting."

"It sounds kind of like a treasure hunt," Michelle said.

"That's what it feels like," Mr. Simon told her. "There are lots of bird-watching groups in San Francisco. They all have websites where you can see what birds have been spotted."

Mr. Simon told the class the names of some of the birding groups and gave their website addresses. He talked about some of the rare birds he had seen. Then he picked up one of the folders from Mrs. Yoshida's desk.

"That's ours!" Rachel whispered to Michelle.

"Let's see what some of you first-time

birders spotted," Mr. Simon said. He opened the folder.

Michelle felt a little nervous. She hoped he could tell what kinds of birds she'd drawn.

"Ah, a rose-breasted woodpecker." Mr. Simon held up the drawing of the woodpecker so that everyone could see it.

Mr. Simon pulled out another drawing and held it up. "A crow," he said with a chuckle. "One of the bossiest birds around. They like to sit very high up and squawk at everything that's going on below."

Michelle relaxed. Her sketches were okay. And Mr. Simon was fun.

The bird-watcher pulled out another drawing. "And here we have a . . ."

Mr. Simon stopped speaking. He stared at the drawing. It was the last bird Michelle had drawn at Rachel's on Saturday, the one with the red markings on it.

Rachel frowned at Michelle. "What's the matter with that drawing?" she whispered. "What did you do wrong?"

"I didn't do anything wrong," Michelle whispered back. "I just drew the bird, that's all. I don't know why he's so upset."

Mr. Simon stared at the sketch a few more seconds. Then he cleared his throat. "Who made this sketch?" he asked.

Rachel pointed at Michelle. "*She* did. We both saw the bird, but *she* drew it."

Thanks a lot, Rachel, Michelle thought.

"This is . . . amazing!" Mr. Simon exclaimed. "Absolutely amazing!"

He isn't upset, he's happy, Michelle thought with relief. But what about?

"This bird is called a Cassin's finch," Mr. Simon told them. "And it's almost never seen in San Francisco!"

"You mean it's rare?" Rachel asked.

"It's rare in this area," he replied. "Where did you see it?"

"Right in my backyard!" Rachel told him.

"Amazing," Mr. Simon repeated. "It's a wonderful sighting. Any bird-watcher would love to say he's seen it—including me!"

Mr. Simon put the sketch down. He slipped a slim book from his jacket pocket and quickly flipped through the pages. Then he hurried over to Rachel and Michelle.

"Is this the bird you saw?" he asked, pointing to a photograph.

Before Michelle could look at it, Rachel snatched the book from Mr. Simon's hand. She stared at the picture for a second. Then she nodded. "This is definitely the one."

"Let me see." Michelle peered over Rachel's shoulder at the photo. It was of a small, mostly dark brown bird with red

31

markings on its head and throat. It did look like the bird she had drawn.

"She's right," Michelle agreed as Rachel gave the book back to Mr. Simon. "That was the bird we saw."

"I can't get over it—a Cassin's finch, right here in San Francisco." He smiled at Michelle and Rachel. "I'm going to post this sighting on my website—with your names. You two are going to become very well known in the bird-watching world—maybe even heroes."

Everybody clapped. Mrs. Yoshida hung Michelle's sketch right in the middle of the bulletin board.

Michelle grinned proudly.

Rachel nudged Michelle in the arm. "This is so cool!" she said with a big smile. "Mr. Simon's putting our names on his website. Everybody will know about us. We're going to be famous!"

Chapter 5

♥ "I still can't believe it," Michelle said to Cassie on the phone later that afternoon. "Who knew that we would actually see a rare bird?"

"It's awesome," Cassie said. "Mr. Simon was really excited. So was Mrs. Yoshida. I bet you're proud that she hung your drawing in the middle of the bulletin board."

"I am," Michelle said. Mrs. Yoshida hung only the best work in the middle. She called it the place of honor. "And that was the last bird I drew in Rachel's backyard. If—"

Before Michelle could finish her sentence, the call waiting sounded. "Hang on a second, Cassie, okay?" she said. "Someone else is calling. I'll be right back."

Michelle pressed a button on the phone. "Hello?"

"Michelle, guess what?" Rachel's excited voice shouted. "A newspaper heard about our bird. They're going to do a story on it—and they want to talk to us!"

"You're kidding!" Michelle cried.

"No, really," Rachel told her. "A reporter called a few minutes ago and told me. My dad spoke to her, too. She wants to talk with us tomorrow after school. It's going to be at my house. And she wants to take our pictures."

"For the paper? This is awesome!" Michelle exclaimed.

"Let's talk about what we're going to say,

okay?" Rachel said. "We should be all ready to answer her questions."

"Good idea," Michelle agreed.

Michelle and Rachel stayed on the phone talking about the interview. When Michelle hung up, she remembered something awful. "I forgot all about Cassie! She's waiting on hold," she said out loud.

Michelle quickly dialed Cassie's number. She wanted to say she was sorry. She also wanted to tell her the good news. The phone rang and rang, but no one answered.

Michelle tried to call Cassie later that evening, but she kept getting a busy signal. I'll see her tomorrow, she thought. She'll understand when she hears about the interview.

On the school bus the next morning, Michelle sat with Cassie and Mandy, as usual. First she told Cassie she was sorry about leaving her on hold.

"What happened?" Cassie asked.

"I was talking to Rachel," Michelle admitted.

"Oh." Cassie looked hurt.

Mandy looked totally surprised. "Since when did you and Rachel start talking on the phone?" she asked Michelle.

"We never did until yesterday," Michelle said. She explained about the newspaper interview. "I just got so excited, I forgot about everything else. Rachel and I talked about what we're going to say and everything."

Cassie frowned. "Michelle, you know Rachel is going to turn into a snob once this bird story is over."

"Maybe. Maybe not," Michelle said. She wasn't sure. Strange as it seemed, she was starting to like Rachel.

"Come on," Mandy argued. "Rachel was nice before so that you would do all the work. Now she's being friendly because she's getting her name in the paper. She knows it's all because of you."

"You might be right. But my dad says that I should at least give her a chance," Michelle said. "Anyway, I'm really sorry I left you on hold, Cassie. I didn't mean to. I'll never do anything like that again."

The bus stopped, and Rachel climbed on. "Michelle, look!" she cried. She waved a sheet of paper in the air as she rushed down the aisle.

"What is it?" Michelle asked.

Rachel sat down in the seat across from Michelle. "It's a newsletter from the San Francisco Bird-Watchers. My dad found it on the Internet this morning and printed it out. Here, read it."

Michelle took the paper. She read the head-line: SCHOOLGIRLS SPOT CASSIN'S FINCH. Then she read some of the story:

"Michelle Tanner and Rachel Tilly, fourth-graders at Fraser Street Elementary School, wowed the San Francisco birding world with their sighting of the rarely seen Cassin's finch."

The story went on to talk about the bird. It was usually seen in the mountains, in spruce and fir trees. The males often flew and sang together. And a Cassin's finch could sound like other birds if it wanted to.

The story had comments from excited bird-watchers, including Mr. Simon. Mr. Simon said that he and his group looked for the finch in Rachel's backyard, but they didn't find it. Now they were searching in all the parks.

Michelle glanced at the beginning of the

story again. It was so awesome seeing her name in print like that.

When they got to school, Mrs. Yoshida pinned the newsletter on the bulletin board next to Michelle's sketch. Michelle couldn't help sneaking peeks at it all morning.

"I can't wait to tell everybody at home about the newsletter," she told Cassie and Mandy on the way to lunch.

"They'll be really happy for you," Mandy said. "Oh, I almost forgot! I got the new Ginger Girls CD yesterday. Why don't you and Cassie come over after school so we can listen to it?"

"Great," Cassie said.

"Definitely," Michelle added. "I can't wait to hear it."

"Michelle, you can't go to Mandy's house today," Rachel said. She and Sidney were walking behind Michelle.

"Huh?" Michelle turned around. "Why not?"

Rachel laughed. "We're being interviewed for the newspaper, remember?"

Michelle almost dropped her lunch bag. "I can't believe I forgot!" she said. "Sorry, Mandy. I guess I'll have to miss it."

Mandy shrugged. "That's okay."

When they reached the cafeteria, Rachel turned to Michelle. "Come sit at my table today. We can talk about what to wear and how to do our hair for the newspaper photo." Rachel and Sidney went straight to their usual table.

Cassie turned to Michelle. "You're not going to eat lunch with *her,* are you?"

"Well . . . I really need to," Michelle said. "Maybe we can all sit together today."

Cassie shook her head. "No way."

Michelle didn't want to hurt her friends'

feelings, but couldn't they understand how important this was? "I'm being interviewed for a newspaper," she explained. "I want to look good."

"I don't get it," Mandy asked. "Rachel is always so mean. Now you're acting like you want to be best friends with her."

"I am not," Michelle argued. "You and Cassie are my best friends. I'm going to sit at Rachel's table only this one time—to get to know her."

Michelle looked over at Rachel's table. Rachel waved to her.

"Besides," Michelle went on. "Maybe Rachel isn't as bad as we thought she was. I mean, she almost seems . . . nice!"

Chapter

6

♥   After school Michelle hurried home to change clothes. Rachel had said at lunch that she thought they should wear dresses. But Michelle hadn't agreed. She said that since they were going to have their picture taken in the tree house, jeans and T-shirts would look better.

Rachel didn't even argue. She actually said, "Good idea, Michelle."

Cassie and Mandy will be amazed when I

tell them, Michelle thought. I really think we were wrong about Rachel.

Michelle put on a pair of light blue jeans and her favorite pink T-shirt with the little daisies on the front.

When she got to Rachel's house, Rachel was waiting for her at the front door. "Wait until you see what I got for us," she said. "Come up to my room. And hurry. We only have a few minutes before the reporter gets here."

Michelle quickly followed Rachel up the stairs and into Rachel's bedroom. Whoa, she thought, looking around. It's so big.

The room was huge. It had a big bed with a white canopy, lots of shelves with books and stuffed animals on them, and a thick blue carpet on the floor. Rachel even had her own television. Arthur, the cockatoo, sat on a perch in his cage near a window.

At home Michelle shared a bedroom with her sister Stephanie. She usually didn't mind, but sometimes it got kind of crowded. She couldn't imagine having a room this big all to herself.

"Your room is awesome," she said to Rachel.

"Thanks." Rachel hurried across the room to the bed. Two white T-shirts were lying on it. She picked one up and turned around. "Look at this!"

Michelle blinked in surprise. "That's my sketch of the Cassin's finch," she cried, pointing to the picture on the front of the shirt.

"Yup! And see what else." Rachel turned the T-shirt around. On the back was Michelle's name in big pink letters. Rachel picked up the other shirt. "I have one, too," she said.

"How did you do that?" Michelle asked.

"I got the idea after you said we should wear T-shirts," Rachel explained. "So I borrowed your drawing from Mrs. Yoshida. When I got home, my mom and I rushed out and got the shirts made."

"I love them, Rachel," Michelle said. "They're going to look great in the picture."

This is getting to be so much fun, she thought. There was no doubt in Michelle's mind. Rachel could be really nice sometimes.

The doorbell suddenly chimed.

"That's the reporter!" Rachel exclaimed. "Let's hurry and put on these shirts. It's time for our interview."

The two girls quickly changed into the matching T-shirts and ran back downstairs. "Hi, I'm Jenny Ames," said the woman at the door. She pointed to a young man with a camera who stood next to her. "This is Mike, my photographer. And you two must be the ones who saw the Cassin's finch. Fabulous T-shirts."

"Thanks," Rachel said. "I got them made just this afternoon."

"Great idea." Ms. Ames took a small notebook out of her jacket pocket. "Why don't we do the interview out near the tree house? That's where you were when you saw the bird, right?"

"Right," Rachel said as they all walked around to the backyard. "It's my tree house. My father built it for me just a couple of weeks ago."

"How nice." The reporter flipped some pages in her notebook. The four of them sat cross-legged on the ground at the bottom of the tree. "Okay, let's get started," she said. "Why don't you start by telling me how you happened to be looking at birds in the first place?"

"It was for homework," Michelle added. "I had no idea I was drawing a rare bird."

"Well . . . yes, but there was more to it for me," Rachel said. "I watch birds all the time. So it wasn't anything unusual for me. I'm always on the lookout for rare birds."

That's not true, Michelle thought. Rachel didn't seem to care about the birds at all that day. But then Michelle decided that maybe she was wrong about that. She didn't know Rachel very well. Rachel might have just been tired. Maybe she really did love birds.

The interview went on. Michelle tried hard to remember all the details of that morning. She wanted to get everything right for the newspaper story.

But Rachel hardly let her speak. She interrupted whenever Michelle tried to talk. And she didn't want to talk about the Cassin's finch, either. Whenever the reporters asked

about the bird, Rachel changed the subject—
to herself.

She went on and on. "I always come up
here to this tree house. It's my bird-watching
spot. I get up early to see the best birds."

Michelle was confused. Why was Rachel
acting that way? She's probably so psyched
that she doesn't realize what she's doing,
Michelle decided. After all, we're going to be
famous.

Then the photographer asked Michelle and
Rachel to climb into the tree house for their
picture. "Okay, give me a big smile," he said.

Michelle grinned as he snapped the picture.
Being famous was definitely something to be
psyched about!

Chapter 7

♥ Wednesday morning, Michelle stood on her front porch and peered down the street. The newspaper should be there any minute. She could hardly wait to see the story about her and Rachel and the Cassin's finch.

I'll ask Dad to buy a bunch of extra copies, she thought. I'll definitely want one for my scrapbook. And Dad will want one of his own. So will Joey and Uncle Jesse. And I bet Mrs. Yoshida will put a copy in the middle of the bulletin board!

When Michelle heard the *squeak-squeak-squeak* of the paperboy's bicycle, she ran down the porch steps. The paperboy waved and tossed the newspaper toward her. Michelle caught it, waved back, and ran inside.

"It's here!" she shouted, dashing into the kitchen.

"Great!" Stephanie said. She pushed aside her bowl of cereal. "Let's see."

Michelle slipped the newspaper out of its plastic bag and spread it on the table. Of course, they weren't on the first page. That was for big-time news.

She flipped the pages until she came to the part that had news about the city. "Wow!" she gasped. There was the photograph of Rachel and her on the very first page of the city section.

"Great picture," Stephanie said. "You look really good, Michelle."

"Thanks." Michelle quickly began reading the story to herself:

"When Michelle Tanner and Rachel Tilly climbed into Rachel's tree house last Saturday morning, they were normal fourth-graders doing a homework assignment. Now they're celebrities."

The article quoted Rachel describing how she looked for the birds. Then it quoted Michelle saying how she drew them and how she had no idea that the last bird she sketched was anything special.

Michelle stopped reading. Maybe I should have told Ms. Ames about how my red pencil broke, she thought. And how I finished drawing the bird with a regular pencil. That might have been a good thing for the story. Oh, well. It's too late now, Michelle decided. It's still a good story. She continued reading.

Next, the article quoted Mr. Simon. He had

been interviewed at his office. He talked about how long it had been since anyone had seen a Cassin's finch in San Francisco. "We see plenty of common house finches," he said. "They're often confused with the Cassin's finch because of the similar red coloring."

The story was continued on another page. Michelle quickly turned to it.

"The house finch has red on its forehead and throat. It also has red on its back and even more on its chest," Mr. Simon said. "The red on the Cassin's finch is only on the head and throat. That's what sets it apart."

Michelle gasped. This was terrible! Horrible!

She and Rachel had made a big, big mistake. The bird they saw *did* have red on its back and chest! Michelle remembered it perfectly. The only reason she didn't keep coloring it was that her red pencil broke.

I didn't think it would matter, Michelle thought. But it matters a whole lot. We saw a regular house finch—not a rare Cassin's finch.

Rachel and I aren't celebrities at all. We're total fakes!

Chapter

8

A few minutes later Michelle got a ride to school with her father. It was faster than the bus, and she wanted to have plenty of time to talk to Rachel.

She's going to be really upset, Michelle thought. But I have to tell her so we can decide what to do.

Michelle hurried into the classroom. Rachel wasn't there yet. Michelle sat at her desk and nervously watched the door.

After a few minutes Cassie and Mandy and

some other kids from the bus arrived. Rachel wasn't with them.

"Is Rachel still out in the hall?" Michelle asked Cassie and Mandy.

Cassie shook her head. She looked a little hurt that Michelle was asking about Rachel.

"She missed the bus," Sidney told Michelle. "Her mother will drive her. She'll probably be here in a few minutes."

Michelle groaned.

"What's wrong?" Mandy asked.

"Everything!" Michelle said.

"Uh-oh. You sound really upset," Cassie told her. "What's the matter? Maybe we can help."

"You mean you're not mad at me because I've been spending time with Rachel?" Michelle asked.

"Well . . . not too mad." Cassie grinned.

"Come on, we're your best friends. Of course we'll help."

"What's going on?" Mandy asked.

Michelle glanced around. "Let's go out in the hall," she said. "I don't want anybody else to hear—not yet."

"This must be super serious," Mandy said when they were in the hall.

"It is," Michelle told her. She glanced around again. "Rachel and I didn't see a Cassin's finch, after all," she whispered. "We saw another kind of finch with red coloring. Only that finch is about as rare as . . . as . . ."

"Never mind. We get the picture," Mandy told her. "But what happened?"

Michelle quickly told them the whole story. "When I read what Mr. Simon said in the newspaper, I nearly fell on the floor!" she said. "Everybody thinks we saw a special bird, but we didn't. What should I do? Should I tell Mr. Simon?"

Cassie nodded. "You have to."

"All the bird people deserve to know," Mandy said.

"I guess you're right." Michelle sighed. "I just feel so awful about it."

"But it wasn't your fault," Cassie said. "You just made a mistake, that's all."

"Cassie's right," Mandy agreed. "Just tell the truth. Mr. Simon will be disappointed, but he'll understand."

"You're right," Michelle said. She had to tell the truth no matter how embarrassing it was. "Thanks, guys."

"There's Rachel now," Cassie said. She pointed down the hall. "I guess you should tell her first."

Michelle sighed again. This is not going to be fun, she thought.

Cassie and Mandy went into the classroom. Michelle stayed out in the hall. Rachel hurried toward her, waving the newspaper over her head.

"Did you see the story?" she asked Michelle. "Our picture is so big! Isn't it great? Do you think my hair looks okay in it?"

"Rachel, I have to tell you something," Michelle said quickly. She took a deep breath. Then she told Rachel what had happened.

Rachel stared at her. "Is this a joke?"

"No! I wouldn't joke about this," Michelle said. "Face it—we drew the wrong bird."

"*You* drew the wrong bird, you mean," Rachel reminded her.

"But it was your idea for me to finish the sketch with a regular pencil," Michelle said. "And you're the one who told Mr. Simon we saw the bird. I know it's partly my fault, but it's not *all* my fault."

58

"Okay, okay!" Rachel crumpled up the newspaper and stuffed it into her backpack. "This is a total disaster!"

Michelle sighed. "How are we going to tell Mr. Simon about this?"

"Tell Mr. Simon?" Rachel gasped. "We can't do that."

"What do you mean?" Michelle asked. "We have to tell him the truth."

"No, we don't. I mean, not yet," Rachel said. She began to pace back and forth. "Okay, let's think about this. Just because we didn't actually see the bird doesn't mean it isn't around."

Michelle was confused. "Well, I guess there could be a Cassin's finch here somewhere. But the only reason all the bird people are looking for it is because we said we saw one. But we didn't."

"Maybe you didn't, but *I* did," Rachel said.

"I saw one at Golden Gate Park two weeks ago."

"You did?" Michelle asked in surprise.

Rachel nodded excitedly. "Of course, I didn't know it was a Cassin's finch then. All we have to do is go to the park and find it ourselves. Then we won't have to tell Mr. Simon anything."

Michelle frowned. "I don't know, Rachel. It would probably be better just to tell everybody what happened."

"Not if we don't have to," Rachel argued. "If we see the bird, then our story isn't a lie! We can go tomorrow—it's a half day."

"But Golden Gate Park is so big," Michelle said. "How are we ever going to find one little bird in it?"

"It can't be that hard," Rachel declared. "We'll just hike around. I'll bring a great picnic lunch. It'll be fun!"

Rachel really wants to do this, Michelle thought. And she's actually been pretty nice to me. We're almost friends, and friends should help each other.

Besides, if there was a chance to find that bird, Michelle felt they should take it.

"Okay, Rachel," Michelle said. "Let's do it. Let's go to the park and find that Cassin's finch."

Chapter 9

♥   On Thursday the girls had a half day, so Rachel's mother picked them up at school and dropped them off at the park. She told them to call when they were ready to leave. "Have fun," she said as she drove away.

Michelle stared into the park. It was huge, with miles of trees and grass and ponds. Are we really going to find a little Cassin's finch in there? she wondered.

"Let's get started," Rachel said. "Maybe we'll be lucky and find the bird really fast."

"That would be great," Michelle told her. "Where did you see it?"

"Oh, it was in some trees," Rachel said. "But it's probably not in the exact same place anymore. Come on. We'll keep an eye out while we walk."

Rachel marched off, wearing a yellow backpack. Michelle followed behind her. She wore Joey's binoculars around her neck.

"There's a bird," Rachel called out, pointing to a tree branch.

Michelle didn't even have to use the binoculars. "Rachel, that's a blue jay," she said. "It's the wrong color, and it's way too big."

"Oh. Right." Rachel kept walking. "Well, don't worry. We'll find it. There's another bird—look!"

The bird Rachel pointed to was small enough. It might be the Cassin's finch,

Michelle thought. Michelle quickly raised the binoculars.

"Well?" Rachel asked eagerly.

Michelle shook her head as the bird came into focus. "I don't know what kind it is, but it doesn't have any red on it at all."

The two girls kept walking through the park. Everywhere they went, they saw birds, but never the right bird.

"Whoa, I'm starting to get tired," Michelle said after a while. "Maybe we're doing this all wrong."

"What do you mean?" Rachel asked.

"I think we should go to the exact place where you saw the bird," Michelle told her.

"But I told you that it probably won't be there anymore," Rachel said. "Birds do fly around, you know."

"Sure. But I think we should start there, anyway," Michelle said. "Maybe it has a nest or something. You said it was in some trees, right?"

"Right, but . . . now I'm not so sure," Rachel admitted. "I mean, it was two weeks ago."

"Try to remember," Michelle said. "Was it in a tree or not?"

"Yes. I mean, no," Rachel said. "Oh, I don't know. What difference does it make? It's not going to be in the same tree now, anyway."

"But it might be in another one close to it," Michelle said. "Think, Rachel! Close your eyes and try to picture it."

"That won't work," Rachel declared.

"It might," Michelle told her. "If you picture it in your mind, you'll remember how you found it. Maybe it was flying toward a tree or hopping around in the grass or . . ."

"I don't remember!" Rachel cried. "Closing my eyes won't help!"

Michelle stared at her. What was with Rachel, anyway?

Rachel sighed. "I'm tired, too," she said. "Let's take a break and eat lunch, okay? Then we'll both feel like looking some more."

Lunch sounded good to Michelle. She was tired and hungry. Nearby was a big pond with a bunch of geese swimming in the middle of it. She and Rachel walked over and sat down on one of the wooden benches.

Rachel had brought cheese, tomato, and sprout sandwiches on pita bread in her backpack. "This looks great," Michelle said. She took a big bite.

"Honk . . . honk!" Two of the geese paddled toward the shore.

Michelle giggled. "They want some lunch, too." She broke off some pieces of bread and tossed them toward the pond. "Come and get it!"

"Honk . . . honk . . . honk!" Three more geese began paddling toward the shore.

The first two geese climbed out of the water and snapped up the bread crumbs. Then they waddled toward the bench. Rachel tossed some bread, too. Then the second group of geese climbed out of the pond.

"Whoa!" Michelle cried. "These birds are hungry!"

Rachel and Michelle couldn't throw the bread fast enough. The geese just gobbled it up.

More geese waddled toward the bench, honking and flapping their wings. *"Honk . . . honk!"*

"I'm out of bread," Rachel said. "I think they want more food."

Michelle nodded anxiously. But she didn't have anything left to give the geese, either. "Sorry, guys, no more," Michelle told the geese. "Time to go back to the lake."

The geese stared at them. Then, one by one, they flapped their wings. They honked even louder than before. *"HONK . . . HONK . . . HONK . . . HONK!"*

Michelle covered her ears to block out the sound. Maybe it wasn't such a good idea to feed the geese, she thought.

Rachel did the same thing. "I think they're mad at us," she said in a panicky voice. "What should we do?"

The angry geese flapped their wings harder. They waddled even closer.

"Run!" Michelle shouted.

Michelle and Rachel raced away from the bench as fast as they could. The honking geese followed them. They flapped their wings angrily.

The girls ran and ran until they couldn't hear the geese anymore. When they finally stopped, they found themselves in a big wooded area. The trees were so thick that it was almost dark.

"The geese aren't following us anymore," Michelle said breathlessly.

"Thank goodness," Rachel panted.

Now that Michelle felt safe, she began to laugh. "That was close."

"Definitely," Rachel agreed. She stared up into the trees. "It sure is quiet. Let's get out of here."

"Wait, Rachel," Michelle said. "Maybe this is the place where you found the Cassin's finch. A rare bird might like it in a quiet place like this."

"I already told you I don't remember where I saw the bird," Rachel said.

"But you're not even trying," Michelle complained. "We'll never find the Cassin's finch this way."

"I'm leaving," Rachel said. "Tell me how to get back to the lake."

"Okay, okay." Michelle sighed. She glanced around, trying to find the path back to the lake. But all she saw was grass and trees.

Michelle gulped. She had been so busy running away from the geese, she hadn't even thought about where she was going. Now she wasn't sure how to get back!

"Well?" Rachel crossed her arms in front of her chest. "Which way do we go?"

"I—I don't know." Michelle shook her head. "Rachel, I think we're lost!"

Chapter 10

♥   "Lost!" Rachel shrieked. "We can't be! How are we going to get back?"

"Don't panic, Rachel," Michelle urged her. "We'll get out. We just have to think of a plan, that's all."

"But I'm too scared to think!" Rachel cried.

Michelle glanced around again. She couldn't even remember which direction they had come from. "Look around, Rachel," she said. "Does anything look familiar from the last time you were in the park? After all, we could be in the exact same spot where you saw the Cassin's finch."

"Nothing looks familiar," Rachel declared.

"You didn't even look," Michelle said.

"I don't have to. I've never seen this place before," Rachel said. "I've never even been to this stupid park before!"

"Huh?" Michelle frowned. "Did you just say you've never been to Golden Gate Park?"

"Yes," Rachel admitted. "I never saw that dumb bird here because I've never been here. I made the whole thing up. I kept hoping we would find it. Then we wouldn't have tell the truth. We could still be famous."

"I don't believe this!" Michelle said angrily. "I let you talk me into looking for a bird you never saw. How could I be so dumb?"

Rachel didn't say a word.

"I wouldn't be lost in the woods now if we

had told the truth right away," Michelle said. "That's what Cassie and Mandy told me to do. I should have listened to them! They're my real friends. You just pretended to be. You're a big liar!"

Rachel still didn't say anything. She just kept staring around. Her eyes were wide. Michelle noticed that Rachel was shivering. And it wasn't even cold.

Whoa, Michelle thought. Rachel is really scared.

Suddenly Michelle wasn't angry anymore. She even felt a little sorry for Rachel. Rachel wanted to be famous so much that she had lied. And now she was so scared that she couldn't think.

"Let's worry about the bird later," Michelle said to Rachel. "The main thing now is to get out of here."

"But we can't!" Rachel cried.

"Yes, we can," Michelle declared. "And I'll figure out how."

"What are you going to do?" Rachel asked in a shaky voice.

"What my dad said to do if I ever got lost," Michelle declared. "Look for a police officer."

Rachel stared at her. "Here?"

"We're not in the wilderness," Michelle repeated. "It just feels like it. Golden Gate Park has park rangers and police and all kinds of people working in it. Come on. Let's find one of them."

Michelle grabbed Rachel's hand and began walking. Soon they found a path. Michelle suddenly realized that the trees weren't so thick. She peered ahead and saw a clearing. "Rachel, look!" she cried.

Standing in the middle of the clearing was a man wearing a tan uniform and a big hat. He was talking into a walkie-talkie.

"A park ranger!" Rachel cried. "We're saved!"

Rachel and Michelle dashed through the trees and into the clearing. "We are so glad to see you!" Michelle exclaimed.

The ranger smiled at them. "What's the problem?"

"We're lost. Can you please get us out of here?" Rachel asked.

"I'll be happy to," the ranger said. "We're not far from the duck pond."

He led Michelle and Rachel through the trees to a narrow hiking trail. The trail took them back to the huge open space.

Rachel pointed to the other side of the big grassy area.

Michelle saw benches they'd run past as they had tried to escape from the hungry geese. She knew where they were now. After thanking the ranger, Michelle and Rachel hurried to pick up their lunch bags and throw them out. Then they started walking toward an arrow pointing out of the park.

Suddenly Rachel gasped. She stopped.

"What's wrong?" Michelle asked.

Rachel pointed to a group of people in the distance. They were walking across the grass toward them. As they came closer, Michelle could see that they all wore binoculars around their necks.

"It's Mr. Simon and a bunch of bird-watchers," Rachel whispered. "I don't think they saw us yet. Quick, let's duck into the woods and hide until they're gone. Then we can figure out what to do."

"No way," Michelle said. "I already know what to do. It's time to tell the truth."

Chapter

11

♥ "Come on, Rachel." Michelle took hold of Rachel's arm and pulled her toward the group of bird-watchers. "We can't wait any longer. We have to tell them the truth."

"This is going to be the worst moment of my life," Rachel muttered.

"Just remember that it was a mistake," Michelle told her. "We didn't do anything wrong on purpose."

"Michelle, Rachel! Hello!" Mr. Simon

called out. He pointed to the other people with him. "These are some of my bird-watcher friends. We're all hoping to find the Cassin's finch in the park today, since no one has seen it in Rachel's yard."

The three women and four men smiled at Michelle and Rachel. "You two were so lucky to see it," one of the women said. "I wish I had been there."

Mr. Simon laughed. "Didn't I say you'd be heroes?" he told the girls.

Michelle glanced at Rachel. But Rachel wasn't beside her anymore. She was standing behind her, trying to hide.

I guess I'm the one who has to tell them, Michelle thought. She took a deep breath. "Mr. Simon, we're not really heroes."

"What do you mean?" he asked.

Michelle took another deep breath. "We didn't see the Cassin's finch."

The group of bird-watchers grew very still and quiet.

Michelle wished she could disappear. But she made herself tell the story. "The bird we saw did have red markings on it," she said. "But—"

"But Michelle's red pencil broke while she was coloring it," Rachel said quickly. "Michelle drew all the birds."

Michelle rolled her eyes. Rachel wants to make sure they know who colored the bird wrong, she thought. She still can't admit that she made a mistake, too.

The bird-watchers didn't say anything.

"Anyway, I just did the rest of the bird with a regular pencil," Michelle continued. "And when you showed us the picture in the book, I thought it was the same bird we saw. But then I read the newspaper article. And I remembered that the bird we saw had a lot more red on it. I guess it was a house finch."

Michelle stopped talking. Mr. Simon and the other bird-watchers were staring into the trees.

Michelle felt terrible. They're so upset, they won't even look at me, she thought. I didn't think they would feel so bad. "We're really sorry," she told the bird-watchers. "We didn't mean to fool you or anything. It was a mistake."

The bird-watchers kept staring at the trees.

Why don't they say something? Michelle wondered. She glanced at the trees and then back at the bird-watchers.

Now they were all looking through their binoculars. What was going on?

"Mr. Simon?" she said.

"Shhh," he murmured. "Stay very still. Very quiet. Do you see it?" he asked one of his friends.

The woman nodded. "Absolutely amazing!"

Wow, Michelle thought. Wouldn't it be great if they had actually spotted a Cassin's finch? "Do you see one?" she whispered. "A Cassin's finch?"

Mr. Simon shook his head. "It's something much more incredible!" he whispered excitedly. "It's a Eurasian kestrel—a type of falcon. And it's a bird that has never been seen here before!"

On Friday at school Michelle told Mrs. Yoshida and the rest of the class the truth about the Cassin's finch. Mrs. Yoshida totally understood. So did everybody else.

Rachel didn't say a word. She acted as though she had nothing to do with it.

Michelle didn't care. She was just glad it was over. Besides, the bird people practically forgot about the Cassin's finch after they saw the Eurasian kestrel. There was a story about it in the morning paper. Mrs. Yoshida cut it out and pinned it on the bulletin board.

"I still like birds, but I'm glad the bird project is finished," Michelle said to Cassie and Mandy at lunch. "I can't believe I actually thought Rachel was my friend. You guys were right. She wanted to be friends only when she thought we were famous."

Cassie nodded. "As soon as she found out the truth, she wasn't your friend anymore."

"That's what you said would happen," Michelle admitted. "I should have listened to you."

"Next time we'll make you listen," Mandy said with a grin.

"Don't worry." Michelle laughed. "There won't be a next time."

Rachel hurried over to their table. "I just

thought of something, Michelle," she declared. "That newspaper story about the kestrel left out a very important fact."

Michelle frowned. "What?"

"Well, if it hadn't been for us, those bird-watchers would never have been in the park looking for the Cassin's finch," Rachel said. "So they would never have seen the kestrel. They should be thanking us. And our names should be in that story. We have got to call the paper!"

Michelle could hardly believe it. Rachel was still trying to be famous. "No way," she said.

"What?" Rachel squawked.

"We had nothing to do with finding the Eurasian kestrel," Michelle told her. "You can call the paper if you want to, but leave me totally out of it."

Rachel stared at Michelle for a second.

Then she turned and marched back to her table.

Michelle knew Rachel was angry, but she felt too good to care. The bird-watchers had seen a really rare bird. And she'd told the truth about the Cassin's finch.

The best part was that she wouldn't have to hang out with Rachel anymore. Doing projects with a fickle friend like Rachel was, well . . . for the birds!

It doesn't matter if you live around the corner...
or around the world...
If you are a fan of Mary-Kate and Ashley Olsen,
you should be a member of

MARY-KATE + ASHLEY'S FUN CLUB™

Here's what you get:
Our Funzine™
An autographed color photo
Two black & white individual photos
A full size color poster
An official **Fun Club**™ membership card
A **Fun Club**™ school folder
Two special **Fun Club**™ surprises
A holiday card
Fun Club™ collectibles catalog
Plus a **Fun Club**™ box to keep everything in

To join Mary-Kate + Ashley's Fun Club™, fill out the form
below and send it along with

U.S. Residents – $17.00
Canadian Residents – $22 U.S. Funds
International Residents – $27 U.S. Funds

**MARY-KATE + ASHLEY'S FUN CLUB™
859 HOLLYWOOD WAY, SUITE 275
BURBANK, CA 91505**

NAME:_____

ADDRESS:_____

_CITY:_____ STATE:_____ ZIP:_____

PHONE:(____) _____ BIRTHDATE:_____

1242

FULL HOUSE™
Michelle

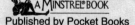

A MINSTREL® BOOK
Published by Pocket Books

1033-35

Don't miss out on any of
Stephanie and Michelle's
exciting adventures!

FULL HOUSE™
Sisters

When sisters get together...
expect the unexpected!

 A MINSTREL® BOOK
Published by Pocket Books

2012-05